Snowman

Guido Van Genechten

meadowside
CHILDREN'S BOOKS

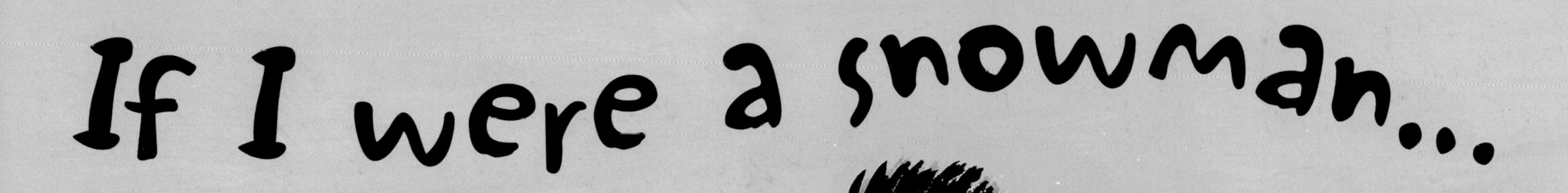
If I were a snowman...

I'd play
snowball in the park,

skate on the ice

and
stand
on my
head!

I'd slide down the snow slopes,

dance
all
night

and SHOUT out loud!

I'd sing
the noisiest
snowman songs,

and give you **BIG HUGS** to keep us warm!

I'd paint
the dottiest
snow paintings,

and watch you
having fun in
the snow.

I'd stand in the sun
and if, one day,

it got
too
hot...

I'd ask all my friends
to make me again!

Meadowside Children's Books
185 Fleet Street
London
EC4A 2HS
www.meadowsidebooks.com

This edition published 2007

A CIP catalogue record for this book is available
from the British Library
10 9 8 7 6 5 4 3 2 1
Printed in Indonesia